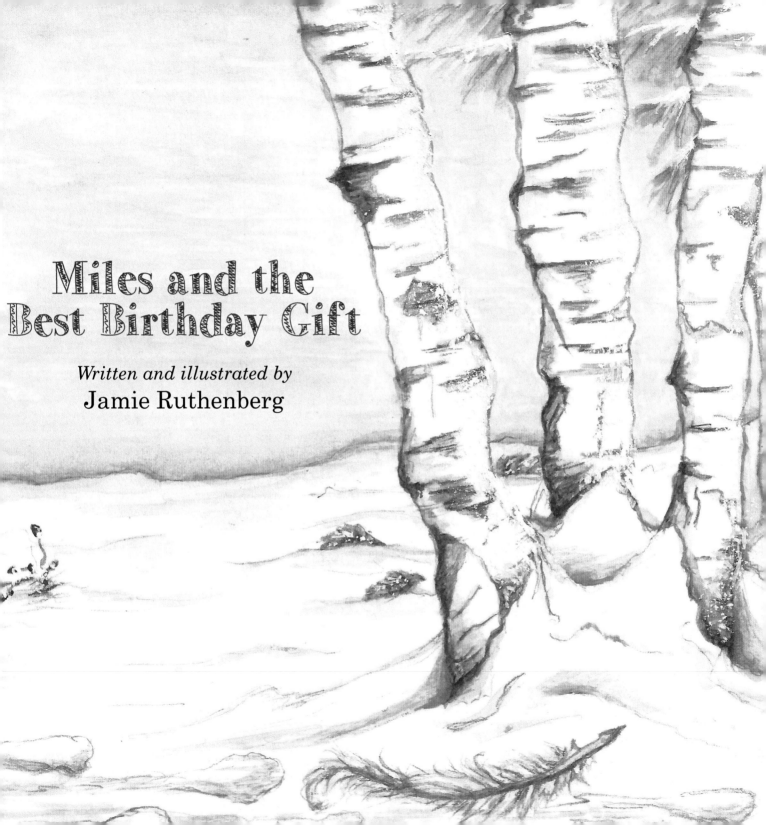

Miles and the Best Birthday Gift

Written and illustrated by
Jamie Ruthenberg

ISBN-13: 978-0692896143

ISNB-10: 0692896147

For my brother,
Jason

It was an early winter morning when Miles rubbed his eyes and sat up in his snug bed. He looked toward the frosty bedroom window and thought of his friend, Violet, who lived on the other side of the pond behind his house.

"It is Violet's birthday today," he said to himself with a sleepy smile.

Miles could not wait to help his mother make the birthday cake for the party at Violet's house later in the afternoon. It was their birthday gift to Violet.

Miles walked over to his bedroom
window, wiped a circle of frost from
the glass, and peeked out. There was
something magical about winter on
snowy days like this.

The whole world was white with
thick, fresh snow. Miles could see the
pond as a sea of snowflakes fell from
the sky, blanketing tree branches and
pines, and hiding the pond's thick ice.

Miles felt the warmth of the room as he walked into the kitchen. He could smell the embers crackling in the fireplace as his mother was preparing to make her chocolate cake with thick layers of rich chocolate frosting for the party.

Cocoa, flour, sugar, vanilla, cream, and butter covered the table as snow still fell outside the window. The oven was heating, the fire was flickering, and Miles felt cozy to his toes.

Suddenly, there was a knock at the back door. It was Violet and her brother, Gabriel!

"Hi there, Miles," Violet said cheerfully, as Mama let them in the door. Violet shook the snow off of her ears and nose. "Gabriel is staying at your house this morning while I go with my Mom to ballet."

"You can help us make the chocolate cake for the party, Gabe!" Miles said with a big smile.

Violet smiled and said, "By the time the cake is done, it will be time for my birthday party! You can help them bring the cake to our house!" Excited, Violet hugged Gabriel, waved goodbye to Miles and his mother, and pranced out the door and into the haze of falling snow.

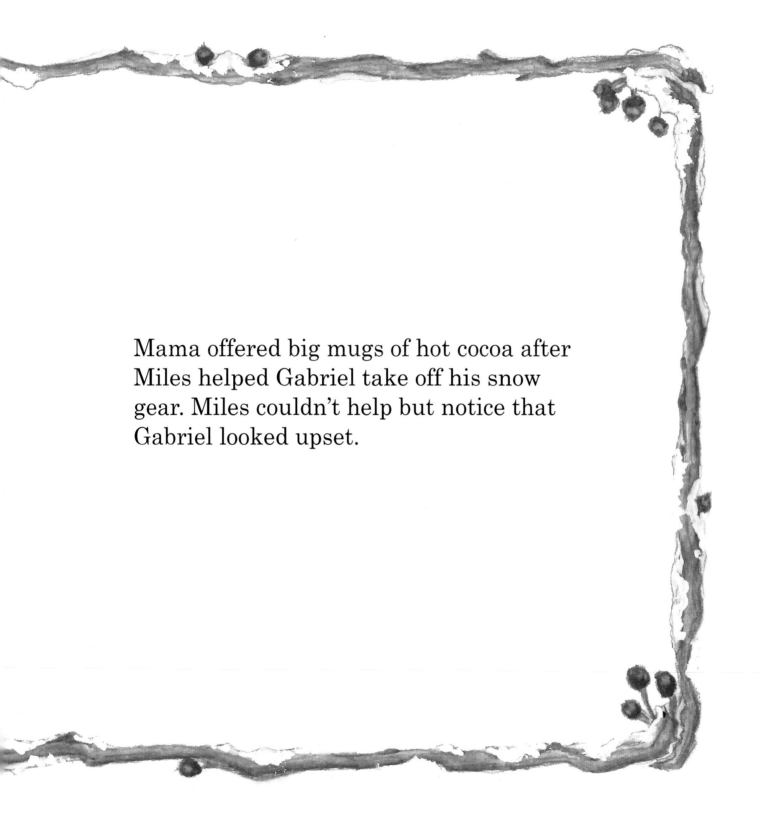

Mama offered big mugs of hot cocoa after
Miles helped Gabriel take off his snow
gear. Miles couldn't help but notice that
Gabriel looked upset.

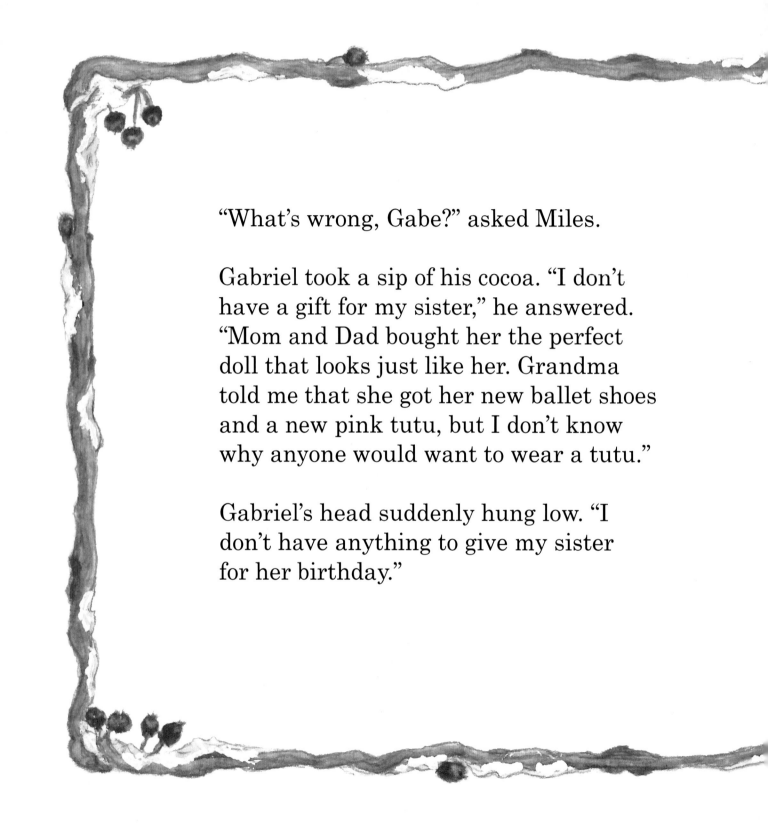

"What's wrong, Gabe?" asked Miles.

Gabriel took a sip of his cocoa. "I don't have a gift for my sister," he answered. "Mom and Dad bought her the perfect doll that looks just like her. Grandma told me that she got her new ballet shoes and a new pink tutu, but I don't know why anyone would want to wear a tutu."

Gabriel's head suddenly hung low. "I don't have anything to give my sister for her birthday."

Mama asked Miles if he would grab logs from the backyard for the fire. So Miles walked through the snow to the back woodpile, all the while thinking about how he could help Gabriel.

Suddenly, Miles heard a deep, familiar voice. "Why the heavy heart, my friend?"

Miles looked up and saw his friend, the Snowy Owl, perched on the branch of a tall birch tree. He had not seen the owl since last winter.

"Hi there," said Miles. "My friend, Gabriel, doesn't have a birthday gift for his sister. Today is her birthday party and he is very upset because he never bought her a gift."

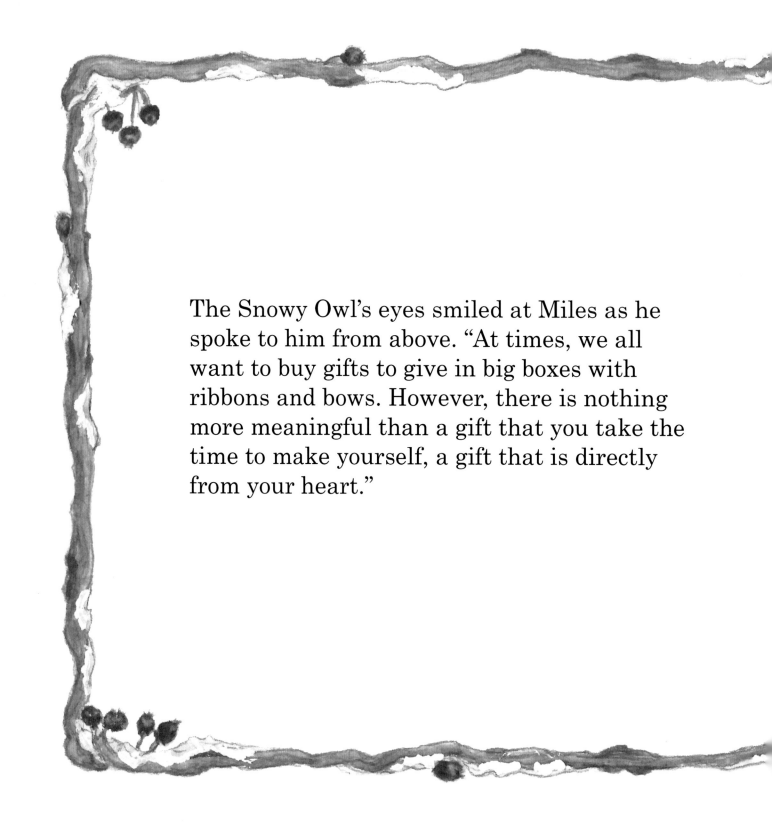

The Snowy Owl's eyes smiled at Miles as he spoke to him from above. "At times, we all want to buy gifts to give in big boxes with ribbons and bows. However, there is nothing more meaningful than a gift that you take the time to make yourself, a gift that is directly from your heart."

Miles looked up at the Snowy Owl as he spoke. Then...

Miles had an idea.

After thanking the owl, Miles walked back with the logs and set them by the fire as he told Gabriel his idea.

"You could write a poem, telling Violet what you love about her," Miles said with a smile.

Gabriel looked worried. "I don't know how to write yet, and I'm not good at rhyming."

"Poems don't have to rhyme," Miles said. "The words just have to sound nice together, like notes in a song. Besides, I can write the words for you."

Miles found his favorite pencil and a piece of paper from his special notebook. Then he sat and helped Gabriel write his poem.

A Poem For My Sister
by Gabriel

Every morning I see you first.
You wake me up
and pour milk in my oatmeal.
You help tie my shoes
and hold my hand when we walk to school.
You eat my peas when Mom is not looking
(don't say that out loud)
and make silly faces when I feel sad.
You like to dance.
You like to laugh.
You like to smile.
When you smile
I smile.
I wouldn't want anyone else to be my sister.
I love that you
are you.

The cake was finally frosted and decorated. Miles and Gabriel walked in the tall snow while his mother carefully carried the cake.

They walked through the back woods and over the ice-covered pond to Violet and Gabriel's house.

Later that afternoon, it came time for Violet to open her presents. The very last gift she opened was Gabriel's. When she read the poem, she paused a moment. Then she gave her brother a big hug.

"This is the best birthday gift anyone has ever given me. Thank you," said Violet, as she squeezed Gabriel.

Hi!

I am writing you a letter again because I really love to hear what you think!
- Did something like this ever happen to you? What happened?
- Have you ever felt like I did in the story, or like Gabriel or Violet did?

Sometimes stories are like other stories.
- Did you ever read a story like this one?
- What was the story? How are they alike?

I hope you write me back soon!
                    Your friend,
                    Miles

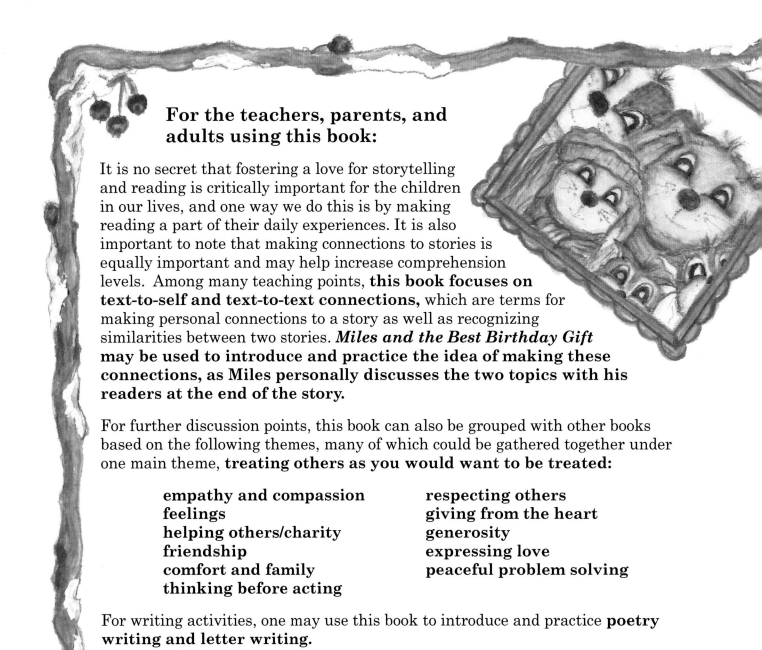

For the teachers, parents, and adults using this book:

It is no secret that fostering a love for storytelling and reading is critically important for the children in our lives, and one way we do this is by making reading a part of their daily experiences. It is also important to note that making connections to stories is equally important and may help increase comprehension levels. Among many teaching points, **this book focuses on text-to-self and text-to-text connections,** which are terms for making personal connections to a story as well as recognizing similarities between two stories. *Miles and the Best Birthday Gift* **may be used to introduce and practice the idea of making these connections, as Miles personally discusses the two topics with his readers at the end of the story.**

For further discussion points, this book can also be grouped with other books based on the following themes, many of which could be gathered together under one main theme, **treating others as you would want to be treated:**

empathy and compassion **respecting others**
feelings **giving from the heart**
helping others/charity **generosity**
friendship **expressing love**
comfort and family **peaceful problem solving**
thinking before acting

For writing activities, one may use this book to introduce and practice **poetry writing and letter writing.**

My Personal Connection to
Miles and the Best Birthday Gift

I'll tell you a secret. Mama's luscious chocolate cake with chocolate frosting in *Miles and the Best Birthday Gift* is actually my recipe. In fact, all of the recipes so far in the series have been some of my favorites to make in the kitchen.

Why put recipes in a children's book series? Seems odd at first. However, family and friends that know me expect it. They know I not only love to create stories and art. I also love to create food! Truthfully, if I care about you, you will know because I will feed you…a lot.

As it is in Miles' home, the kitchen was the heart and soul of my household while growing up, and it has remained that way for me into my adulthood. It is one of the ways I spend time with the people I love, and one of the ways I show love. It's how I unwind and center myself. It's what I do when I am extremely happy, or especially upset. It's how I deal with life.

So I'm sure it is no surprise that my absolute favorite birthday gift to give someone is the birthday cake! The image of Miles' mother carefully carrying the cake, lovingly made that morning, to Violet's party is reminiscent of the countless times I've done the same. There is nothing more heartwarming than watching someone's face light up when walking through the door with his or her favorite cake, homemade and from the heart. Miles and his mother know this all too well.

—Jamie Ruthenberg

Every year, I make the exact cake Miles' mother makes as a gift for my daughter, Gracie. It's her absolute favorite! My little niece, Noelle, feels quite the same. She did all she could to resist sticking her finger into the frosting (I didn't think she was going to make it), while waiting patiently for a piece of her birthday cake.

About the Author

Jamie Ruthenberg is a Detroit-born author and illustrator, as well as a professional writer and certified teacher. Today she lives in Clarkston, Michigan with her daughter, Gracie, and is working on the next book in the Miles series, along with a young adult series based on the same heart-warming themes.

Jamie has been sketching the character of Miles since she was a small child. Many years later, with watercolor and pencil, she has developed him into a kindhearted and thoughtful soul that treats other with love and respect, even during challenging circumstances. He is truly a character with integrity that treats others as he would want to be treated.

by Jamie
Ruthenberg
AUTHOR / ILLUSTRATOR

Artist's note:

The paintings for this book were created with pencil and watercolor.
The text was set in Century Schoolbook.

If you enjoyed this book by Jamie Ruthenberg, you and your family may also enjoy another one of her delightful stories!

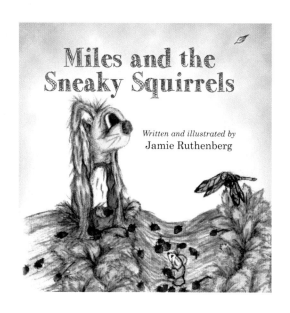

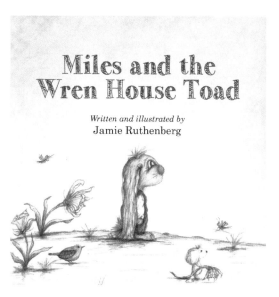

Miles and the Sneaky Squirrels Paperback ISBN: 978-0692486054
Miles and the Wren House Toad Paperback ISBN: 978-0692704509

Available for purchase at:
JamieRuthenberg.com (signed copies)

Made in the USA
Middletown, DE
03 August 2019